CW01635151

In The Year 2066
True-Life Sketches

read. enjoy - pass on.

Leave your comments on:

davemahoney@live.nl

boek·scout

Eerste druk © 2021 David Mahoney

Coverafbeelding: © Kelly Rekveld
© maodoltee – Adobe Stock

ISBN: 978-94-645-0130-8

Uitgeverij Boekscout Soest
www.boekscout.nl

David Mahoney

IN THE YEAR 2066

True-Life Sketches

In The Year 2066

Latest news headlines from the BBC.

A hundred years on from the signing of the International Covenant on Civil and Political Rights; the year in which the Beatles were more popular than Jesus (according to John Lennon), the year in which England triumphed in the World Cup Final and the year that many baby boomers regard as the true start of the sexual revolution, another historic milestone has been reached. Today the ruling Liberal Democrats booked a resounding victory in both The House of Commons and the decimated House of Lords. The Law states that all women over the age of 16 have an undeniable right to an orgasm. 90% of the Lib. Dems, 75%being female MPs voted in favour and only 40% of the opposition voted against the new Law.

Gone are the days of women having to fake an orgasm purely for the sake of massaging the male ego – or to prevent outbursts of anger due to a burst pride or even being blamed for an erectile dysfunction. The ball, no pun intended, is now in the other court.

This Law specifies that all males over the age of 16 must have a clear understanding of the intricacies of the female body and mind, thereby creating an emotional equality in which mutual satisfaction is an inalienable Right. Failure to uphold this universal Right of women may result in a four-figure fine or a compulsory training on female sexuality.

Finally we can banish the word "frigid" from the dictionary. Pornography will no longer be the learning tool of growing male adolescents and women will no longer have to live with the threat of rape hanging over their heads.

Also in fashion, subtle changes will begin to take place as women need no longer adapt to, or even protest against the conformity imposed by male hegemony.

Women's Lib has finally become Women's liberation.

Mary Glynnis-Smythe.
Political Editor at the BBC

Final Score

John arrived home in a foul mood. His date with Maria hadn't gone as he had planned. The morning itself hadn't started well as his wife had confronted him with her suspicions, which obviously he had denied, but it had led to a mother of all arguments. It just didn't seem fair that nowadays a man couldn't go through his mid-life crisis without having to face a Guantanamo Bay interrogation. He had hoped that Maria would console him and give him another chance to practice his love techniques. And what happened? She dumped him. Their relationship wasn't going anywhere she said. What a load of codswallop. "Not going anywhere!" They'd only done it once for Heaven's Sake. All in all a morning to forget.

He tramped around the room, grabbed a beer from the fridge, shouted at the cat and finally settled down to watch the World Cup semi-final: England against Germany.

After the first goal for England his mood became noticeably lighter. The second and third goal made him forget all the day's sorrows and he was positively rapturous when his wife walked through the door five minutes after the final whistle. He took her in his arms while singing "You'll Never Walk Alone" and kissed her with gusto (although to him he was being passionate).

She felt that he was begging her to forgive him. Obviously she had no proof that he was playing away from home but a woman's intuition never lets her down, does it? Even so she felt the old familiar stirrings low down in her body and decided to just forgive him and clear the air with a few minutes of intimacy and, having squared it with her conscience, she returned his advances.

John couldn't believe his luck. He undid her blouse and bra and jumped over the sofa to close the curtains, while managing almost simultaneously to remove his trousers and boxer shorts. He didn't even complain when he saw that his wife had settled down on the sofa on top of his new West Brom home shirt. He closed his eyes and imagined Maria's breasts in his hands while "boing, boing the Baggies" played in his mind followed after a few minutes with "can we play you every week?". Finally to the tune of 'We are the Champions" he let out a sigh of relief that was probably audible all the way to the Hawthorns.

Extricating his Albion shirt form under his wife's bottom, he went to the fridge for another beer. And in this post-coital frame of mind he counted his blessings. His marriage was salvaged, England in the final of the World Cup and tomorrow he'd give Maria a ring… one never knows, does one?

Je 'taime

Valentine's Day was swiftly approaching and the hints Jane had been dropping were anything but subtle. They'd been a couple -she liked to call it "romantically involved" – for 15 months 3 weeks and 2 days. To him it felt a bit longer.
Gordon was a happy-go-lucky type of fellow who enjoyed the simple pleasures in life such as fishing, going down to the pub with his mates, barbeques in the summer and skiing in Scotland in the winter. He had just signed up for three years in the Royal Navy and while celebrating this rite of passage the barmaid, Jane, gave him a free pint and her telephone number. Not one to turn down a free pint and chivalrous as he was, he said thanks and wrote down his number on a coaster, subsequently forgetting the whole episode. Two days later, however, while packing his hold-all for his trip to Portsmouth, Jane phoned him. She said that she'd been told that he had joined up and that she would still like to see him again. Although there were no butterflies in his stomach there also weren't any alarm bells ringing in his head and he agreed to go out for a meal when he came home on leave. One thing had led to another and now after 15 months, 3 weeks and 2 days he was out of his depth.
Gordon had never been prone to delve too long on his feelings. Self-analysis cost too much energy and any assertiveness he may have been born with had been knocked out of him by his father who had embraced the philosophy of spare the rod and spoil the child. His mother on the other hand had smothered him with her love for herself. Obviously not the best foundation on which to build a long-lasting relationship based on true love and understanding.

He thought he ought to blame himself for allowing this fling with Jane to have got out of hand. Fair enough, he liked her and she was brazen in bed and willing to learn. Unfortunately he could no longer envisage returning from a three month mission abroad to be greeted by Jane with all her uninteresting bits of tit-tat. Moreover, the idea of visits to her family and evenings out with her friends was a positive nightmare.

While on watch on his last night on board he had managed to do a bit of soul-searching. It was time to unravel the knot he'd tied for himself.

When he joined up he had imagined that he would be able to show his prowess in the face of adversity. A true hero should he have to fight for his country. Patriotically cheering having sent an enemy ship and all its crew to the bottom of the sea. But now he had to face up to dumping Jane.

Two hours into his watch, in the small hours, a solution manifested itself.

He would send her a bunch of flowers on Valentine's Day and attach a self-written poem to it. This would prevent any embarrassing scene in a restaurant and in a couple of days she'd silently thank him for the effort he'd put into letting her down softly.

Je 'taime

She opened my brain and asked:
Do you still love me?
But my right lobe was out of order
And my left one could not find the words
Which the vocal cords were expected
to prepare for emission.
Till finally
The sun's rays entered the exposed organ
And the power of speech returned.
Air was inhaled, nasally of course
And was held in check
Till the tongue and lips were sculptured
And the necessary exhalation took place
Causing that wondrous talent
Which separates man from beast
And the word "no" became audible.

Dear Jane,

I wrote this for you. I thought it was better this way. Maybe one day we'll meet again as friends. Thanks for the 15 months, 3 weeks and two days.

Gordon

Orange Juice and Coffee

Dear Diary,

After three weeks of being nursed in St. Bridget's Institution for Mental Health I need to share my feelings with someone who really understands me. I didn't mean to take an overdose but when I received Gordon's flowers, note/poem my lights went out. Why did he treat me like that? I don't think he truly realized how much I loved him.

I still don't understand how I could have been so forward that first night in the pub. He just seemed so strong and sensitive and interested in me. As you know I've never been good around guys. Always felt too insecure and being politely plump didn't help. And neither was becoming tongue-tied whenever a boy struck up a conversation with me. But Gordon was different. I'd tell him things I'd never shared with anyone but you. When he came home on leave he'd listen to me in such an understanding way. When we visited my parents or went out with my friends he was always incredibly considerate. He didn't join in the conversations much but he said he felt at home around them.

I gave myself 100% to the relationship even (this is embarrassing) experimenting with his more bizarre sexual fantasies. Losing my virginity to him seemed completely the right thing to do. Occasionally I would mention, in passing, marriage and babies at which his lips would curl up into a little smile. What was I not seeing?

After he had left on his latest mission I was so heart-broken that I wrote him a poem. I should have realized that something was wrong as he never reacted to it. And then to receive that poem… I was devastated. He hadn't even written it himself. It was a poem our

English teacher had used to explain the mechanics of language formation.

The flowers hit the kitchen wall first and the poem ended up shredded in the wheelie-bin but the darkness in my mind was terrifying. It seemed never-ending and that's why I swallowed the bottle of pills. I suppose I ought to be glad that mother came around for an unexpected visit, which she does four times a week. And now here I am. I've been signed up for counselling and I'll be off the anti-depressants in a couple of months. One thing I do know for certain is that one day my love will turn into hatred and my depression will turn into anger. It will only be then that I'll be able to pick up the shreds of my life again.

Orange Juice and Coffee

"Don't worry love
we'll meet again" he said.
Before the customs gate became a barrier
And she could only wave and brush away her tears.
Dreading having to return home
To tax her feelings to the limit.
Each tear was an emotional earthquake
And at each sigh she forfeited two pints of hope.
John and Paul had described her "yesterday":
Languishing in his arms,
Satisfied,
Sweated and sperm-ridden
After a night of saying goodbye.
The inevitable, nourishing breakfast of
Two fried eggs, sunny side up
Toast and marmalade,
Orange juice and coffee.
The flood gates held in place
By naïve wishful thinking
Till the isolation of the shower
Brought partial relief.
The packing had the subtlety
Of medieval torture;
Every item laid carefully
In its own place,
Represented another turn of the screw.
Why had he packed her soul?

Why couldn't he have left her a little bit of life?
Was it the true meaning of "give and take",
When only one gave and the other took?
You bastard… goodbye my love
And yes, please God! Let us meet again.

The last lesson

Boys and girls, finally, we have arrived at our last lesson together. I have enjoyed the two years I was allowed to be your English teacher but now the time has come to say goodbye. Many teachers hand out chocolates or self-made cards during their final lesson but I'd like to give you something more tangible: one of life's lessons in the form of a short story based on an old Buddhist folk-tale. I can't prevent you from making mistakes on your life's path; and I wouldn't want to because they are your greatest teachers, but as we all know, forewarned is forearmed. Sit back, listen and allow me to hand over your present.

One bright Spring early morning a dog decided to go for a walk in the forest. The sun's rays were just making their way through the trees and there was a crispness in the air that gave him that "good to be alive" feeling.
He hadn't gone far when he saw a baby bird lying on the ground. It had probably thought that it was time to spread its wings. Unfortunately, they weren't strong enough and he ended up nose-diving to the ground and breaking both of them. The dog decided to take the little bird with him and look for help. He carefully picked him up in his mouth and continued on his walk.
Despite the dog's good intentions this turned out to be a harrowing experience for the little creature and his heart started beating ten to the dozen. "The poor chap's not going to survive this" thought the dog to himself and he decided to find a comfortable place for him to spend his last few minutes.
At that point he'd reached a field full of cows who'd produced enough cowpats (dung to you non-agricultural lot) to give him a choice of resting place for the bird. Gently he placed him in the nearest cowpat. It being a warm and soft place for him to pass away peacefully. With a final goodbye the dog went on his way.

But lo and behold, the warmth of the cowpat sent a spurt of life through the little bird's body and he began to chirp softly. Chirp, chirp.
Close by, a fox was just waking from his morning nap and he was feeling a bit peckish. He heard the tweeting and went to investigate. When he saw the little bird he was somewhat disappointed as it wouldn't satisfy his hunger but it would do as a snack. He took the bird out of the cowpat, licked it clean and: swallow, swallow, gone! …

The moral of this story ladies and gentlemen is: it's not always your enemies that drop you in the shit and it's not always your friends that pull you out of it.
There's the bell for the end of our final lesson. Thank you and goodbye.

The M-Spot

Ladies and gentlemen,

Welcome to our 15th annual congress of sexology. As you are aware posters portraying new ideas and discussion points are arranged in the main hall. Many, if not all of them will be of great interest to us who are engaged in the therapeutic side of sexual behaviour. I would like to introduce you to our key-note speaker, Professor Jaap Miedema from the University of Groningen in the Netherlands. Jaap, together with his team of researchers, has made a break-through discovery. Unfortunately Jaap will only have time to give a short presentation due to the fact that the Thalys waits for no man nor woman. Jaap hardly needs any introduction as we all know him through his ground-breaking work with victims of female genital mutilation. He personally has been responsible for many countries in the Sahel region passing laws prohibiting F.G.M.. Today, however, he will return to his original expertise: the male and female orgasm. Ladies and gentlemen. Jaap Miedema...

Thank you Charles, it's a great pleasure to be here among you again, even if my time is somewhat limited. Although my theme today is male sexual stimulation, our research in Groningen owed much to the discovery of the g-spot in 1981 by the German gynaecologist , Ernest Grafenberg. Notwithstanding that his research showed that this "so-called" g-spot is only traceable in approximately 1 in 10 women the consequences were enormous. Despite the clitoris remaining the main focus of female sexual stimulation this extra possibility has broadened the scope of our work. Coincidentally it also

caused tremors in various religious communities both eastern and western. Many church leaders secretly expressed their concern. How could women be kept subdued if science were to keep making these kind of discoveries? Forgive me, I'm getting side-tracked.
Our hypothesis, formed a number of years ago, was that there must be corresponding areas in both male and female bodies. That being the case, where is the corresponding g-spot in men? I'm proud to be able to disclose today that we have managed to detect its whereabouts. Due to the male preoccupation with penetration it was probably inevitable that tunnel vision would occur, also among scientists. We decided to broaden the horizon so to speak and investigate the generalities rather than the specifics. It was revealed to us by chance, as is often the case in scientific discoveries.

One of our female volunteers had broken her middle finger while cycling and she was unable to bend this particular digit. While trying to stimulate her partner by cupping his testicles, her middle finger automatically made circular motions a bit higher up which gave him even more pronounced sensual feelings the like of which he had never experienced before. We did further tests in a controlled laboratory situation and without a shadow of a doubt we had discovered a new erogenous zone. A group of nerve endings midway between the scrotum and the anus about half a centimetre in diameter. We've dubbed it "the m-spot".
Ladies and gentlemen I truly believe that with the g-spot and the m-spot in our tool kit we will be able to achieve a much higher success-rate percentage among our clients. For example our estimation is that roughly 90% of all cases of psychologically-based erectile dysfunctions can be remedied.
I had prepared an extensive power point on our findings, unfortunately time and travel restrictions mean I have to curtail my presentation. However, should you wish, the power point will be available

on-line through the usual channels as of Tuesday next week. And our paper will be published in the Lancet on Monday
Thank you for your time and the genuine interest you have shown. I apologise for not having the time to answer the questions you inevitably have but I promise to make an appearance at next year's conference.

I'm off to catch a train. Goodbye and see you next year.

The Convent Girl and the Inner City School

Alice had always known that she would become a teacher. As a young girl she used to place her teddies and dolls on the bed and read to them and tried to teach them their ABC. However, it was only after she began to teach English at a Comprehensive school that it became painfully aware that fantasy and reality are not always interconnected. At 29 she had become one of the statistics of young teachers who had fought and failed; principles and ideals trampled in the mud along with the pearls of wisdom she had tried to pass on to a new generation.

Her parents were staunch defenders of the loyalist propaganda opposing Catholic emancipation yet they were emancipated enough themselves to send their daughter to what used to be a convent school in England. On the demise of the last nun, the Order had sold it and it had been turned into a non-denominational boarding college. Originally it was meant to be co-educational but the board of Governors soon realised that a girls-only establishment was the preference of the rising suburban Middle-Classes. There were many boarders from Northern Ireland as there was a great fear for their health and safety – not to mention their virginity, which was of course never alluded to.

Academically speaking Alice couldn't have asked for a better preparation for a future teaching career but it definitely didn't prepare her for life in the real world.

Alice's year group was an incredibly like-minded group of girls. A most exceptional occurrence according to their tutors. They were studious and never rebellious. Alice herself described it as a home from home but without the parental pressure. Obviously the girls did have night-time discussions in the dormitory about boys and what would be expected of them as wives. Generally speaking, however, they were more into *Wuthering Heights* than either *Histoire D'O* or the bourgeoisie of the Bloomsbury group.

English had always been her favourite subject and it surprised no one when she chose to read English at Durham University. At the ripe old age of 24 and with a 1st Class teaching degree in her satchel she plunged into the next phase of her life truly believing that the world was her oyster. Her parents had tried to persuade her to return to Northern Ireland and after giving it some thought finally rejected the idea as not being conducive to the life of liberty she had planned for herself.

Some people take to teaching like ducks to water. Alice was not one of those lucky ones. In retrospect she should have chosen a more sheltered environment to take her first steps in teaching but being filled with a crusading spirit and a wish to improve young people's lives she chose a large Comprehensive in Newcastle. To say she was shocked at the moral fiber of the young people entrusted into her care would be putting it mildly. Nevertheless she soldiered on as she had inherited her father's stubbornness and her mother's resilience.

Despite all her preparation work and self-reflection her lessons were quite often chaotic. The pupils weren't inclined to listen. On the other hand they never reacted to her personally as they were wont to do with other teachers. They just couldn't be bothered wasting their precious hours at school by learning English. Listening to how they spoke to each other, Alice couldn't help believing that her lessons would actually be very useful to their development. Away from Newcastle they would be unable to have a conversation of any profound length of time. Her worst hours were teaching year 10. One could feel the hormones raging through the classroom and every time they opened their mouths, which was incessantly, the only subject they were capable of talking about was various parts of the anatomy and their respective mechanical possibilities. Her attempt to instill in them a certain maturity by using all her didactic powers and trying to be a role model was doomed to failure.

Two closely related events finally led to her downfall, her ultimate dismissal and the last push over the edge of insanity.

The first was a heavy blow even though it only resulted in a mild reprimand. On the curriculum for year 10, Shakespeare and poetry were an important part of the syllabus. When discussing the Renaissance she happened to mention in passing that the rose was in fact a symbolism of the female sexual organ citing certain passages from Shakespeare's plays. Unfortunately one of her pupils was called Rose who for the next weeks was tormented by all the boys in the class calling her "fanny" whenever she walked by. Rose's parents wrote a letter of complaint which resulted in the Principal reprimanding her.

The second event was painful to her personally as it was a direct challenge to how she saw herself as a teacher. After having seen the film: "Dead Poet's Society" she believed avidly in the power of poetry. Wasn't it John F. Kennedy who had said: "When power leads man toward arrogance, poetry reminds him of his limitations. When power narrows the area of man's concern; poetry reminds him of the richness and diversity of his existence. When power corrupts, poetry cleanses"?

She once took her year 10 to the public park to help explain the Romantic Movement and how poets such as Wordsworth were inspired by nature. She gave them an assignment in which they should try to find inspiration in nature and subsequently express their feelings in a poem. All in all she received five letters of complaint from angry parents questioning why she'd done something as dangerous as taking their under-age children to the park with no other teacher going along to help supervise the group. She also received one attempt at a poem:

I'm looking at a tree,

But the bugger ain't looking at me.

It was at this juncture in time that her feelings of despondency really kicked in. Year 10 were the epitome of all that was going wrong. They had also started goading her during the lesson and it was being picked up by other year groups, also the younger ones. It finally all came to a head when she set them another poetry writing assignment. The task was to write a poem about one of the different kinds of love they had discussed while reading *Romeo and Juliet.* Obviously she hoped for a sonnet on courtly love but in its place she was handed in a pile of handwritten trash. There was one poem written by the ringleader of the group, Spike. Later she found out that he himself hadn't written it but he had found it in a contemporary book of poetry.

Animal Knackers

I'm Dan, Dan the dandelion man.
Follow me on a pornographic trip
To Mother Nature's brothel
And a peep show on a ship.

The birds and the bees are busy
The rabbits are doing their best
To populate the dunes and the forests,
A good example to all the rest.

The ducks are raping the females
A gang-bang in the ditch.
The cat has no doubt about Thomas
And a dog is sniffing a bitch.

The stallion stands proud and erect
Waiting patiently for a "yes" from the mare.
His foreplay is meant to appease her
But he only gets an inscrutable stare.

The bull does his work sedately,
Wham, bam and yet another thank you ma'am.
The sheep take off their clothes only
After being serviced by the ram.

The fellatio miming of the fish,
swimming around looking for food,
is an aphrodisiac to many of the impotents,
who use their mind to get in the mood.

The bees collect all of the pollen,
As a sacrificial offer to their queen.
The sweet seed of royal servitude,
The Plebs lick their Regina clean.

The animal kingdom is oh so beastly,
And Mother nature is quite often bare.
Thank God for having invented us humans,
We who walk with our noses in the air.

When she walked into class the following morning and saw the smirks on their faces she literally cried out in anger and accused them of everything she'd managed to keep stored away the last few months. Taking Spikes' poem she read it out loud in a voice full of disdain, tore it into eight pieces and threw the pieces out of the window. The class's reaction was a shuddering jolt to her nervous system. Every depravity they could conjure up was brayed at her. The noise was overwhelming until the deputy head opened the door to find out what was going on and from the one minute to the next the hullabaloo ceased and she could make her escape.

The school decided not to let the problem escalate by punishing the pupils. Instead the Principal gave them a lecture on responsibility and school values. Alice was taken off teaching duties but when more letters arrived from irate parents she was sent home on sick leave. The letter of dismissal arrived three weeks later.

This was the end of Alice's teaching career. Nipped in the bud by an educational system that only has ears for its "shareholders", the parents and managed by people who are only interested in spreadsheets and who need to surround themselves with like-minded weaklings. Alice wrote one final entry in her diary before she threw herself into the path of the intercity to Scotland:

"I was betrayed by a system in which teaching and teachers are not the priority, only good results count. We grade pupils' work but teachers are graded too; not their work but how they adapt to the system. Forgive me for having failed".

Alice, 23 April 2010

Emma's Dream

Notwithstanding her Dutch roots Emma had never been the promiscuous type. She always used to joke that she was Miss Average: in looks, grades and marriage. She'd never been adventurous. A weekend in North Wales on a Duke of Edinburgh's Award scheme was as far as she got and even then she'd become homesick. She'd married young to a man who had shown interest in her at her work and she was now settled in her own home with two children, obviously a boy and a girl, and a husband with whom, once a week, she dutifully made love on a Friday evening. He had his work and his golf and she had her part-time job and her maternal housekeeping role. She'd grown accustomed to it and felt relatively safe within her own confines.

Leading up to her 40th birthday the dreams started. She always referred to them as "the dreams", things which happened to her but were not of her: e.g. her husband being unfaithful, her children on drugs or her daughter pregnant. Sometimes her husband would wake her up because she was screaming in her sleep.

The word "nightmare" comes from Middle English and denotes a female evil spirit thought to lie upon and suffocate sleepers. Emma, however, refused to believe that it was her life that was suffocating her and that the messenger of the night was sending her a warning. Not until that is the dream she referred to as "that Friday Night dream".

She was standing naked in front of a full-length mirror and she knew there was someone behind her, watching her, observing her even. Slowly she applied her lipstick and rouge to her cheeks. While putting on her mascara she looked into the mirror to see who was behind her but her own nakedness blocked her vision. She caressed her breasts, surprised at how hard her nipples were. Moving her hands downwards she felt her wetness and began to rhythmically massage her labia. She felt a sensation which she didn't recognise but which she instinctively knew to be an onset to an orgasm. Then she heard a voice commanding her to stop but her cravings were too strong and she reached her climax. Daring to open her eyes and look again at the mirror she saw God smiling at her approvingly. That is when she woke up, bathed in sweat and the sensation of her orgasm still lingering in both her body and mind.

She got up to have a shower followed by her dream. What was its significance? It seemed as if many of her beliefs had somehow been shattered during the night. It was not her humdrum daily existence which had been mirrored in her dream.

Quite the opposite, it was a different Emma altogether, not this average Emma. Some seed had been planted in her brain and the nagging feeling stayed with her the whole day. That evening she looked up her dream in her Dream Book:

"If a married woman was putting on makeup in front of a mirror, such plot foreshadows new love experiences. It can be both newly resurrected feelings for her husband, or an unplanned love and passionate affair with another man".

She knew that neither was true. She retraced her dream and finally realised that God for whom she had felt such longings and who had aroused unknown feelings in her had the smiling, understanding face of a woman. Her arousal was an awakening to her true self. She now knew without a shadow of a doubt that the man who was always flirting with her at work would not and could not ever be her lover. Maybe, one day, her God would manifest herself and only then would she decide which fork on the two-pronged road she would take.

Soliloquy

Were we in a theatre I would shout out: "is everybody happy?" and everyone would shout back: "yeess!". That's what we do in life: "how are you?". "Oh alright thanks". "How are you feeling?" "Great, yes".

Fortunately here and now there are just the two of us and I believe we should begin to be truthful to each other. I had a look at your Facebook page and was surprised to see how many friends you had. The photos you uploaded were also amazing. If I smiled that much I'd get lockjaw. Also noticeable was the fact of you wearing long-sleeved blouses and t-shirts even when the sun was shining. Why is it we never want to show our true face to the world?

Right, here we go. How are you, really? Doesn't that beautiful smile of yours cover a whole range of other feelings? Isn't it just a facade? All those friends you have – how many were there when the diagnosis came through a few months ago? How many came to hold your hand and comfort you following the operation? And did one of them hold the bowl for you to vomit into?

I was overjoyed to hear that you'd been given the all-clear. I hope you don't mind me saying it to your face instead of re-liking it on social media.

Do you ever share your doubts and fears? The ones you inevitably feel in the wee hours. Or is it only your pillow that dries your tears?

I saw your last post. A photo of you and him raising a glass near the sea front. (Smiling again!). No one would guess that beneath your long-sleeved blouse was an arm full of bruises. "I'm sure I'll be able to change him. He had a difficult childhood".

No I'm not saying you shouldn't be happy. Fake it till you make it as they say but please don't fake it with me. As Peter Sarstedt sang many moons ago: "I know where you go to my lovely, when you're alone in your bed. I know the thoughts that surround you, 'cause I can look inside your head". This isn't arrogance. This is total honesty on the part of both of us. We see each other the way we are, not the way we want others to see us.

I accept your bruises because you have accepted them. I'm pleased at your many friends and smiling photos on Facebook because they make you happy.

When your world crumbles I'll pick you up and support you until you are capable of walking on your own two feet again. Should your friends and your God fail you, I won't.

The love you are so desperately searching for and craving for is right in front of you. I am you. My love for you is infinite. You just need to see it and to embrace it. Take me in your arms and then carry on smiling on Facebook.

At the Psychiatrist

Good afternoon, please come in and take a seat. The guard can wait outside. I'm not anticipating any problems and should anything untoward occur the alarm is in touching distance.

Right John. May I call you John, or would you prefer Mr.Green? Good, okay John. I've been asked to assess your mental health before your trial starts. Honesty on your side could be very helpful to your case. Let me see. You're accused of physically and mentally maltreating your partner with whom you have been in a relationship for 15 years. Is that correct? Okay, whether that is the case is up to the judge to decide. I just have to fill in some background details.
I see in your report that it is not the first time that your emotions have got the better of you. Would you say that you have a problem with anger management John?
In clinical observations of delinquents, as also in clinical DNA trials, a noticeable parity has been established between our biology and our environment. In days gone by, in fact even as late as 2025, it was a choice of nature or nurture. But thanks to ground-breaking research by colleagues of mine in several State Penitentiaries over the last ten years, we now know that the gene or genes have to be present in one's DNA before they can be fuelled by our environment. Your medical file indicates that you would be susceptible to bouts of violence due to a faulty gene. This doesn't automatically entail that you do not have a free choice, and that's where I come in.
Do you get a kick out of kicking, which obviously is a case of faulty wiring, or have you learnt that violence is the only way to express certain emotions? If it is the former, you can expect a "chemical

sentence" viz. a custodial sentence during which period you will be prescribed medicine to alter your DNA. However, should the latter be the case then it will be the judge's prerogative to sentence as he or she sees fit.
Tell me about your childhood John. Oh, I see I've hit a raw nerve there, could you extrapolate please.
Right, if I understand this correctly your father would punish you by hitting you with his belt while at the same time saying: "this is hurting me more than it is hurting you". I see and this was a weekly occurrence, was it?
And your mother? Okay, relax, try not to get worked up and just relate the facts. Ehm, yes. She made you feel that you were to blame for all her sorrows: "bringing you into the world was 24 hours of indescribable suffering and it didn't get any better".
Didn't you ever feel love? Oh, only if you did something to deserve it and even then it was short-lived. That must have been painful? And no it couldn't have helped that the first woman who showed you any affection, you made pregnant.
Let's have a closer look at your emotions. Feeling anger and being angry are two entirely different things. When your anger manifests itself you can also choose to ignore it, which you do not do . I see, you just have to lash out. You have to hurt someone or else you yourself might get hurt, is that it? And in retrospect you feel guilty about what you've done. Ehm, unfortunately John, retrospective guilt is a lame excuse for one's inability at prospective action.
Okay, thank you John. We have to end the session here. Thank you for your openness. I will send my conclusions to the Judge within 48 hours. That will provide your lawyers ample time to prepare for next week's trial...

John Green, please rise for sentencing.

After due consideration and careful study of all the circumstances and noticeably the psychiatrist's report, my judgment is as follows: You will be taken to Penitentiary Island where you will remain until the doctors can prove that the medicine has had the required effect. Furthermore, your parents will be banished to the Desert Reservation for a corresponding length of time. Let us hope that one day the moral teachings we have introduced will permeate all levels of our society. Take them away.

The Poet and the Plane Crash

Daniel didn't consider himself to be a window cleaner, he was a poet. Anyone seeing him perched on his ladder wielding his chamois would never guess that, as a teenager, he'd considered a career as a policeman. He wanted to experience the real world to prepare him for his true vocation, that of a poet. Another reason for his choice was his experience of being bullied at school: "hey matchstick, give us a light" was one of the more humorous put-downs. He'd always been a scrawny, shy little boy and his hope was that police training would make a man of him (as his father seemed to repeat quite often). Unfortunately thick glasses and occasional bouts of asthma put paid to his plans.

He'd been writing poetry since he was knee-high to a grasshopper and as he grew into maturity his talent developed accordingly; to such an extent that he had his own blog on the internet on which he uploaded a daily poem. He had a few hundred followers/subscribers who warmly praised his work but it was insufficient to earn a living. He didn't see himself starving in a garret to earn a few paltry pennies. His aim was to open people's eyes to life's realities. Above his kitchen table, where he usually wrote his poetry, he had hung an extract from George Eliot's, *Middlemarch*:

"To be a poet is to have a soul so quick to discern, that no shade of quality escapes it, and so quick to feel , that discernment is but a hand playing with finely ordered variety on the chords of emotions a soul in which knowledge passes instantaneously into feeling and feeling flashes back as a new organ of knowledge."

This became his mantra.
Daniel loved his job cleaning windows. Fresh air, keeping fit by climbing up and down the ladder all day, having a birds-eye view of daily life and, more importantly, the people he came into contact with.
Although he'd been baptised he was no longer a practicing catholic. However, the poetry of the bible had left an indelible imprint on his mind. Occasionally, while meditatively cleaning windows, he'd think of passages from the bible. His favourite at the moment was from St. Paul's Letter to the Corinthians:

'When I was a child I spake as a child, I understood as a child, I thought as a child; but when I became a man, I put away childish things. For now we see through a glass, darkly; but then face to face.

Every day he looked through a glass darkly but he saw his thoughts face to face and these he turned into poems.
His work schedule on a Thursday always ended at a 5-storey block of flats where he had about twenty clients. His favourites were Abdullah in flat 5 who always had a sweet treat made by his unseen wife waiting for him, Charles in flat 10 who kept up a running commentary from inside his flat about how poorly his team were doing and Mrs. Cook in flat 14 where he would always get a cup of tea and a Jammy Dodger.
There were days when he would spend as much time chatting as cleaning windows. He saw that some of his clients were quite lonely. Mrs. Cook, for example had a daughter in The Lake District but she was too busy to come down south too often; "it is quite a journey you know", she would say every week.
In flat 32 an elderly gentleman resided, surrounded by his war memorabilia and yellowed photos on the wall. He never waved, he always saluted and tipped Daniel a pound. Every Thursday he'd be

sitting in his armchair polishing some brass memento. Even though he was old, grey and bent his eyes shone and Daniel always felt strangely happy when they exchanged salutes.

One Sunday in July, round about 5 p.m. Daniel was warming up his evening meal when he heard an almighty bang followed by an eerie silence and then sirens, hundreds of them it seemed. He switched on the television just in time for the news flash: "10 minutes ago a cargo plane crashed into a block of flats 10 minutes after take-off. We'll let you know more as soon as we have an update from our reporter at the scene". And then he saw that it was "his" block of flats! He was paralysed. He could only keep staring at the picture on the television, tears streaming down his cheeks. What had happened to Abdullah, Charlie, Mrs. Cook and his saluting friend in flat 32? The BBC reported that there were no survivors. Where the flat had stood was now a gaping hole. Behind the BBC reporter the viewers could see what remained of "his" block of flats and the cargo plane, which, due to a technical malfunction, had killed his friends.

After a while he changed channels to Channel 4 as the BBC needed their air-time for "East Enders". The reporter of Channel 4 also wore a suit and tie but his accent was colloquial. Another difference was that although the man from the BBC sounded like a funeral director while reporting on the tragedy, his colleague at Channel 4 was more like a ringmaster. At one point he even had the audacity to say that notwithstanding this being a tragedy of great proportion, if the plane had flown on for another 30 seconds a 20-storey block of flats would have been in its way.

This was too much for Daniel. He switched off the television and just stared into space.

Later that evening he took down his card-box, where he kept cards for all occasions. He wrote one card for each of his friends determined to take them to the accident site the day after and to buy a few bunches of flowers on the way there. He did manage to fall asleep but at 3 o'clock he woke up with the words of the reporter ringing in his ears. And he did the one thing he knew would help alleviate some of his pain: he wrote a poem…

The News

S.O.S., S.O.S Mayday, Mayday'
Oh Christ we're going to crash.
No. Fuck. Flats. Oh God, no
We're going down
Mooooooooooooooooom!

But the cameras were quickly there,
The correspondent gave a cough and combed his hair;
For ages he looked for someone crying, with
In the background the sounds of people dying.

"Move that ambulance, it's spoiling the view".
"Excuse me officer, can you spare us a minute or two, to
Tell the viewers all that you know
It's as important as the pictures we're going to show".

That man's lost his son. "Switch on the sound you fool!
We're not paid for silent movies as a rule.
Let's go closer for an award winning shot.
Well, take off your bloody coat, if it's too hot"

"Dear viewers, this is a terrible tragedy;
Well-informed sources expect that there will be
Hundreds of dead. We'll let you know all that transpires.
We'll ask twenty experts and show you the fires".

"Right, let's call it a day and pack up our stuff.
We've been filming for one and a half hours and we have enough
Film for the national news, and if we play our cards right
They'll give us a prize for our work here tonight."

A Love Letter

Dearest Vicky,

Many writers have written that the days drag by when they are not in the presence of their loved ones. I too used to believe that was the case until I met you. My days fly by as you are constantly in my thoughts. The memories we have constructed together are a warm blanket protecting me against the cold, dark hours when we are apart.

Do you remember our walk along the beach last November? It was a rough night, but dry. We may be just two specks of sand in the eternal universe but that night we were the brightest shining stars in the sky. Years after Zeus had split us apart we were finally reunited and neither Aristophanes nor Coleridge had been fully able to put into words the way we felt that night. Our feelings transcended language. Our touches and caresses said more than days of talking. One kiss and an embrace was a journey home.

You are not only my soul-mate you are my be-all and end-all. We don't need defences against the world because we are the world.

I spent the last ten minutes staring out of my window into the night but all I could see was my own reflection. When you're standing next to me I can see as far as the moon and I can count all the stars. When I glance at your face framed in the window tears of overwhelming joy and happiness spring into my eyes.

For the first time in my life I have learnt what "making love" means. It is not an expression of a physical need it is a spiritual fulfillment. While exploring each other's bodies we discovered each other's souls...

An old Indian saying is: *if you love something, set it free. If it comes back, it's yours. If it doesn't it never was.*

I set you free because I love you. I understand the difficult choice you had to make. However, my heart has been opened and there is only room for you. What we have forged cannot be put asunder. Please take my love with you on the road you have chosen. I refuse to use the Future tense when thinking of us as that is for your husband and children, you are my Present.

How to end this letter? "Love"? No it is too clichéd. "Keep well"? We have no say in the matter. "I hope to see you again"? But I see you every day whenever I close my eyes.

No let me finish with one word denoting infinity.

Lemniscate,
Michael

Adultery

An old Chinese proverb says: "there's nothing more attractive to a man than another man's wife." Who then invented monogamy? And even more important, why for God's sake?

I once had a one-night stand with a female colleague which ended in me having to go to hospital with a broken nose and a cracked rib after she had stupidly confessed to her husband. Adultery can be very painful, you know and honesty isn't everything it's made out to be.

Would the world be a better place if we didn't have the institution of marriage? Probably not. Look at what happened in the communes in the 60s and 70s. Free love and a load of jealous hippies preaching love and peace while bashing each other's brains in over a Joan Baez look-alike.

Maybe a somewhat strange analogy but if you have one chocolate éclair it's a pleasure; if you're given the keys to a patisserie you become frustrated and satiated. My philosophy in life is that women want children and female friends whereas men want to have sex and their freedom. It's so simple.

In certain aspects of our lives we are no different to animals. If we are to be honest, and the time has come that we must be, then male mammals have had their day. When, and not if, the day dawns that wars will come to be an unnecessary spillage of energy and lives, men will become superfluous. Look at the stags, stallions and the male in a pride of lions: majestic to look at, protecting the females and cubs from outside aggressors and competing amongst each other for the right to mate. The females patiently wait and subsequently goad the males on with a certain coquettishness and when the deed is done they triumphantly return to the harem while the male sneaks off to his domain. Do lions or stags or bulls or stallions or rams look pleased with themselves after mating? No! They look as if they're suffering from P.M.D.: post mating depression. Even the ancient Romans knew this:

Quod omne animal

Post coitum est Triest.

Evolution has ordained that women no longer need husbands to supply that little piece of DNA which they will turn into their off-spring. In the future there will be stud farms where semen will be harvested and sold to fertile females. Men will be demoted from guardians of the herd to carers and housekeepers.

This male nightmare scenario is already being enacted in certain communities. Not only in non-hetero relationships but more and more also in the traditional households.

Can this male Armageddon be halted in its tracks? Nope, sorry guys the writing's on the wall. How then can we prevent all men turning into lemmings? I believe that solidarity has always been somewhat overvalued and we can't fight evolution. However, let's look on the bright side. And in my opinion there are two bright sides. The first is religion. Christians, Muslims, Jews are all the same. They all believe that God is on their side and they all believe that God is male. That means that until some very brave women stand up and make themselves heard and become the leaders of our planet then wars will still be fought, atrocities carried out, women subdued and marriage institutionalized.

The second bright side is women themselves. They just can't do without us! It is a fact of life that there are certain things that can only be done by men – no, I refuse to do any summing up. The

weaker sex can only exist if there is a stronger sex – or a less weaker sex depending on how you want to look at it. And our female counterparts occasionally need to be in this position, not one of subservience but of vestal virgins lounging in their temples being waited on while offers are made to them.
Adding up the two bright sides results in a third one. The institution of marriage will still go through a period of longevity. Women will still marry in order to procure that much-needed DNA sample albeit belittling the weaklings who they need to produce said specimen. This will result in a longing for strong companionship for them to be able to air their weaker side. Ergo! Gentlemen: adultery guaranteed!

The Zen Vlog on Tuesday

Good morning and welcome once again to my meditation Vlog. To some meditation is sitting in an uncomfortable position, watching your breath entering and leaving your body, even though your eyes are closed, and trying to block out all thoughts. I once heard a joke which was closer to the truth: "don't just sit there doing nothing, go and meditate".

Meditation is a verb. It denotes an activity in which we are 100% present at that particular moment in time. Not to escape from the world but to embrace it. A true acceptance of ourselves "warts and all". You are the way you are and that is good.

We are all searching for the same thing: a return to Love. And love for ourselves is the greatest gift we can bestow, not only on ourselves but also the world.

Don't be afraid of facing up to your feelings. Sometimes they are demons and sometimes they are angels but they are all yours. Say hello and goodbye to them simultaneously. Don't be afraid of fear. Fear is a friend wrongly trying to protect you from yourself. Thank him and send him on his way.

There are only three things needed on your inner journey: courage, determination and perseverance. Take the first step and allow the others to take their designated place. Your final destination will not supply you with your answers, the signposts on your road will. These signposts can be people you meet, occurrences during your daily life, moments of great joy or deep sorrow. Remember that these are your carefully selected package of problems, yours and yours alone. No one else may have the blessings which these problems bring to you. And only you have the special abilities, talents

and wisdom to make these problems your teachers.
Today, for a few moments I would like to zoom in on our free will, and the choices that we make. People who say "I had no choice" are no better than robots. We are all responsible for our actions regardless of the situation we find ourselves in. I'm pretty sure that many of you have been confronted with irreversible actions, either your own or those of others. It is an undeniable fact that we must live with choices which turn out to be irreversible. A plank can be unscrewed but if you've screwed someone you can't unscrew them. There's a famous English saying: "You can't unscramble scrambled eggs". And here is where our free will comes into it.
First accept that you are not perfect. Even you can make mistakes. Look with love on that part of yourself.
Secondly accept that you have hurt someone: consciously or sub-consciously and ask for their forgiveness. Blaming the other person for your actions is a sign of weakness, saying sorry is a sign of strength. When you forgive another person, you forgive yourself.
Let us now close our eyes and look at our inner selves. Breathing in we are at peace and breathing out we smile. Alive to this moment. Repeat…
When you hear the gong, open your eyes and say hello to both the inner world and the outer world, they are one!

Enjoy your Tuesday.

The Envelope

Marjorie lay in bed staring at the alarm clock. In two minutes it would make a hell of a row and she'd have to start her day. She wasn't even comfortable lying in bed as she was wearing an old pair of knickers that were twisted around her bum leaving everything at the front uncovered. She was tempted to let her fingers roam downwards but decided against it. She believed that masturbation should be a slow and enjoyable affair and not the quickies that her ex had put her through the final few months that they'd been living together.

She cut off the hullabaloo of her alarm before it had the chance to really get started. She slouched into the shower to wash away all the nocturnal aromas and to have a pee at the same time as she was trying to save water. Once back in the bedroom she felt she ought to adapt her clothing to her PMS, viz. black bra, undies, trousers and a turtleneck sweater. Keeping in the spirit she also chose red socks and black leather boots.

While getting dressed she heard the letterbox. Thinking that the postman must be on night-shift as he was never this early, she decided to finish doing her face first as it was probably just bills or advertisements.

She was halfway down the stairs when she saw a light-blue envelope lying on the front door mat. I didn't know it was Valentine's Day she jokingly said in herself as she picked it up from the mat and took it with her to prepare her breakfast. Her breakfast menu never changed from one day to the next: instant coffee, a bowl of cornflakes and two pieces of toast and marmalade. It was while she was eating her cornflakes that she opened the envelope – and she nearly

choked. It was a dick-pic and written on the reverse side was: "one day this will be all yours".
Marjorie was a level-headed woman usually but this shook her up no end. She started trembling and crying. The picture itself had already been dropped onto the Formica table top as if it was a piece of hot iron. Looking at the picture she very nearly spewed up. "What is this?", she cried. This was a somewhat silly question as any fool could see it was a photograph of an erect penis. "Who would do this?". Again not a very logical question as it had been sent anonymously. But taking all things into consideration and accounting for her state of mind at that moment one can put the questions into perspective.
Without thinking she swept out the house, got into her car and drove to the police station. As no WPC was available she told, and showed her story to the Duty Officer. "Miss, if this is all you have to go on, I'm afraid there's not much we'll be able to do. I shall write up a report and attach the photograph to it and one of our officers will look into the matter. If anything comes up – and no, it wasn't meant as a joke – we'll be in touch.
Make sure you lock the door properly before going to bed and try not to go anywhere on your own for a while. It goes without saying that you should come and see us if more of these ….ehm… things are shoved through your letterbox. It's probably just a prankster and I'm pretty sure more of them will turn up at other addresses. Just be alert for a while."
Feeling deeply dissatisfied and not at all assured at what he had said she went to work. At least it would take her mind off this shocking experience and she would be able to share it with her best friend at work, Abigail. Who knows, maybe they'd have a good laugh about it.
Much to her surprise and dismay Abigail – Miss Certainty – wasn't at work. Apparently she had phoned in sick that morning, quite

distraught the receptionist said. Marjorie couldn't believe her ears. Abigail was never ill; unlike herself who'd call in sick with a hangover citing hormonal dis-balances. Funnily enough this was always accepted as fact and when she returned to work the following day she would get looks of understanding from her female colleagues and the usual sneers from the men. No, something wasn't right and she decided to go around after work. Obviously she could phone her but then she'd never get any work done.

5.30 on the dot she rang Abigail's front door bell. "My God , you look a mess" she exclaimed when the door was opened. Eyes red and swollen, unwashed and unkempt, Abigail could have posed as a model for a charity organization. On seeing Marjorie she threw herself into a tantrum and blubbered hysterically: "What have you done? Why? I thought we were friends. You bitch. I hate you." This wasn't quite the welcome she'd been expecting and to Marjorie there were two options available: weather the storm and find out what was going on or fire back a retort and go home.

The two women had known each other for donkey's years. And although it was a cliché, they had shared many good times and a few bad times. They'd even dated the same fellow, although not simultaneously, and had a great time comparing how he was with each of them. These talks really raised Marjorie's awareness of men: they are all dickheads, they never change their repertoire, either verbally or sexually, and they really are only interested in two things. Abigail's latest flame was the epitome of all this with one more appalling characteristic which was worse than all the others, he thought he was funny. Finally the tsunami quietened down and in between sobs and barely comprehensible Abigail told her story, while punctuating her narrative with "you bitch". Apparently Jovial Jack had gone for a jog early in the morning and, on his return tried to persuade Abigail to join him in the shower. She, being still sore from the previous evening had refused. Jack didn't do refusals and before he went to

work he'd opened his fly, took out little Willy and said: "it doesn't matter, I've already given this to Marjorie".
Marjorie was gob smacked, livid, murderous and comprehensibly shouted at Abigail what he'd done. It was at that moment that Happy Jack made his appearance. He looked at the pair of them and couldn't stop laughing. Tears was streaming down his cheeks, which was a pity otherwise he would have seen that his hilarity was not being shared and that a certain look had passed between these two she-devils. Also being as the only school he'd attended was the sports school he had never read the quotation from Shakespeare: "Hell knoweth no fury than that of woman scorned".
Literally within seconds he was on his back, hands tied tightly to the oak table and his feet to the radiator. "Come on girls, it was just a laugh. Where's your sense of humour?"
While Abigail pulled his trousers and boxer shorts down to his ankles, Marjorie cut open his t-shirt with the kitchen scissors. "Hey, where's big boy?" Abigail said mockingly, while Marjorie pulled aside her black knickers and peed all over his face. He tried acting tough but once he saw the scissors again he changed tack and began pleading, apologising and promising.
By this time Little Willy, fearing for his safety, shrank to baby proportions. Abigail picked up her phone and took six photos of this juvenile organ. "Pay-back time, Mr. Funny Man", she said as she uploaded the images onto his Facebook account, glad that he had so many friends. She handed the phone to Marjorie who added the text: "One day this could be all yours, unfortunately".
"Time for a drink?" asked Abigail. "Yeah I need filling up again, let's go" and off they went, arm in arm to their favourite pub.

Wednesbury Wives

Alright John, are you coming for a drink tonight? I expected to see you at the match , did something come up? No, okay, yeah sure we'll talk about it down the pub. The match? Bloody useless. They were prancing around like the vicar's croquet team in fancy dress. The centre forward expects the ball to follow him like his dog does and the manager just stands there with his hands in his pocket; he's probably more interested in a game of pocket billiards than getting his team to play as if they'd actually like to win occasionally. We can't complain at losing 4-0, at least it gave the keeper a chance to do something instead of only shouting obscenities at the defenders. All in all I might need more than one pint. Oh, you too? Right see you at the King's Head.

(Before going any further dear reader I should give you a bit of background information. Wednesbury, an old market town, is situated in the Black Country, where men love their wives – wenches as they're called – sport is a popular pastime – pigeon racing, dog racing and football – and there are a lot of folk poets. Strange but true).

Hello mate, go on I'll get the drinks in. You look as if you need one… Right spill the beans.

It's the missis Joe, salt of the earth she really is, but what she did today was sneaky, really sneaky. I think it's because hers going around with that Nora from across the road. Ar, you know her, divorced three times, five kids and works at Sainsbury's. I was having a lie in this morning as last night's pub quiz went on longer than usual and I was still feeling a bit groggy. The missis suddenly put her arm around my waist and started playing with me dick. Hell I thought to myself this is a bit unusual. She then got me to turn over, looked me in the eyes and said: "why don't you go and wash yourself and then come back into bed", at the same time licking her lips. I thought hers gonna gobble me and like a flash I was in the bathroom.

(Break! Dear reader let me explain something about the local dialect. People from deep in the Black Country are known by the sophisticated people from Birmingham as "yamyams". This relating to the fact that they don't say: "are you going to the town"? No, they say: "yam gooin up taan am ya?" We left John explaining the inexplicable actions of his wife that morning. You being reasonably intelligent people had probably already surmised that "to gobble" refers to fellatio. A Black Country man would never stoop so low as to say: "are you going to perform fellatio on me?" No, it would be much more poetical: "Am yo gonna gobble me?" Romance is not dead in The Midlands).

In retrospect I wasn't thinking straight. Well, you don't at moments like that, do you? You know women really can do two things at once. There wasn't that much space left in her mouth but her still managed to say: "hey John, how about going shopping together this afternoon instead of you going to the match? You know they're going to lose and that'll make you feel unhappy. We'll go around the shops instead." Well, you've been roped in haven't you. Hook, line and bloody sinker.
Like I said, salt of the earth but I can't get over this. I ought to man up but you know me and arguments don't mix. I've never had cause to complain, as I said salt of the earth. I'll get another drink in.
You know mate while you were away getting the drinks in and eying up the barmaid I had a think about your predicament. I really think you should do something about them feelings of yours. If not you'll end up with an ulcer. Look, write a poem! You know that one you wrote when the Wolves got relegated and the Express and Star re-

fused to publish it, it was bostin.
(Okay dear reader, this is a colloquial expression meaning that the poem he had written on the relegation of Wolverhampton Wanderers, a football team, was, albeit not at the literary level of other famous writers from The Midlands, viz. Shakespeare, Jerome K. Jerome etc. it was still one that gained a notoriety among certain factions, namely West Bromwich Albion supporters).
Ask Dan Partridge to get it put in the paper. He owes us one for not telling his wife what he got up to at the works Christmas party and he's now become editor at the Star. Let's face it, you've learnt your lesson and it will definitely not happen again. Write a poem and get on with your life.
The following morning John phoned Joe to thank him for his advice and to read him the poem he'd written. Joe couldn't believe his ears and all he could say was: "get it published you twat, it's bostin!".

(Yes, you're getting the hang of it dear reader. Joe considered the poem to be a true reflection of John's feelings. In a nutshell so to speak. You may have difficulties with the word "twat", a non-literary expression denoting the female genitals. It can be used in an unfriendly way, usually to start a fight or it can be used in an amicable way between friends. Whether the poem is "bostin" I will let you judge for yourselves".

Wives

The catholic church allows us
16 wives as you know:
4 better, 4 worse, 4 richer 4 poorer
And maybe one more for the show.

A nurse to look after us when we're ill,
A cook to keep us fed.
A washerwoman who cleans our clothes for us,
And a whore sometimes in our bed.

A nanny to take care of the children,
A friend when we're in need.
A "lady" to take to the party,
A woman who knows how to follow, but also lead.

A mother to give us comfort,
A charwoman who'll keep the house clean.
A partner when having to make decisions,
But a child to be taught what we mean.

A mistress for all of our fantasies,
A fan to fall at our knees.
An object for our anger and frustration
A plaything when we're in the mood to tease.

Yes thank you, Roman catholic church,
For this aid to a better life.
But wouldn't it be a bit simpler,
If we had all these things in one wife?

Guilty

When the judge asked how do you plead? He broke into a smile and with a feeling of joy answered: "guilty!". Yes he had broken into that shop and had stolen a bottle of whisky and a carton of cigarettes. The police found these items displayed in his window-sill when they visited him at his home. He hadn't made it difficult for them to find him either: finger prints, smiling at the CCTV in the shop and driving his own car to the scene of the crime. The judge sentenced him to 240 hours community service and a 500 pound fine. On leaving the dock the thanked the judge who thought he was just being cynical; but he wasn't, on the contrary, he was being totally honest and, unbelievable as it may seem in his everyday life he was a model citizen. "Finally", Gordon thought to himself, "I am guilty of something I really did".

Let's rewind this story to discover what had led up to this stalwart champion of the moral society committing such a felony.

As far back as he could remember Gordon had suffered from a debilitating guilt complex. He was the younger of two brothers, real chalk and cheese siblings. Gordon's aim in life was not to cause waves, whereas his elder brother, Simon was a hurricane. Nowadays he would have been plastered with labels such as ADHD, ADD and one or two others but in those days he was classified as an unruly child and left to his own devices, punished every other day and each evening got sent off to bed after dinner. Gordon always felt sorry for his brother's naughtiness and subsequent punishment and for his mother's cries of: "why are you doing this to me?" and their father's anger – usually after a visit to the pub. He felt it to such an extent that he would try to deflect all these emotions by taking the blame on himself which, for some strange reason, nobody ever believed.

At school it was the same story. He always blushed and looked down at his desk when the teacher asked the class a question such as: "who tacked this worm to the blackboard?". He wouldn't dream of doing such a thing but, unfortunately for him, he was the only one who felt any kind of collective guilt.

During puberty and adolescence rebelliousness did take hold of him but always within his own confines. He tried to make himself scarce when random acts of vandalism or violence occurred within his group. His friends got a kick out of these things, he himself would lie in bed later on sympathising with the victims and never the perpetrators.

This tale of woe continued being a never-ending story when he got married. Every day inter-relational questions would leave him feeling mortified. "Who didn't put the lid on the butter?"; "why is the toilet so dirty?"; "who ate the last apple?".

Finally it got to the point in his life that he felt it was his fault if a car broke down while he was in it. If their plane was delayed he'd say to his wife: "See I've jinxed it again". The proverbial straw was while watching the news one evening together with his wife. A woman had been killed in a hit-and-run accident on the Oxford Turn-Off and he turned to his wife and said: "it wasn't me, honest". Her reaction to this, many would say understandable reaction, was not so much a mirror being held up to him but one being smashed over his head. Her conclusion could also be placed in the "understandable" category: "get help or get lost".

In retrospect it might have been better for Gordon if he'd asked his wife what she meant by getting help. He interpreted it as an ultimatum to start feeling guilty solely for things he himself had done

wrong. The more he thought about this the more liberating it felt, but how to go about it he pondered.
The following day he had an appointment at the barber's. He enjoyed these visits as it meant it gave him the chance to look through magazines he would never buy himself. He picked one up at random and saw that it was a monthly Buddhist magazine which a previous customer had left behind. It was on the front page that he read: "embrace your feelings, don't run away from them". It struck him like a bolt of lightning. Here was the answer to his predicament. His whole life up till then he had felt guilty about things other people had done, it was time to experience true guilt…….. Two days later he broke into his local off-licence.

Extract from Gordon's memoires. Page 324
The episode I recounted briefly in the previous chapter was my catalyst to change. My experiment backfired but also propelled me forward. Without it I would never have achieved the status I enjoy and would never have become one of the world's leading bankers. Nor enjoy the jet-set, globe-trotting life which is now my due. For the first time in my life I had done something in order to feel actual guilt and much to my surprise, I didn't feel any guilt whatsoever. Likewise six months later when my wife and I divorced, I felt no guilt at her recriminations and accusations. Yes, they were all true but my spirit had been freed.
While still actively involved as CEO at the bank, the so-called "white-wash affair" as also the "junk mortgage affair" were like water off a duck's back. I had needed neither a psychiatrist nor a mumbo-jumbo practioner to bring about this change. It was all thanks to that one sentence in the magazine to which I am still a subscriber in acknowledgement of its influence on my life; that one sentence was: "embrace your guilt!".

Live Life to the Full

Good afternoon and welcome once again to our series of webinars entitled: smiling from cradle to grave, sponsored by Light Pharmaceuticals.

First let us recap briefly on what was discussed in the first webinar. All of us know people who look as if they got out of the womb the wrong side. However, regardless of what life throws at us we all have a choice how we face up to life and last week we saw that laughter definitely is the best medicine.

It all starts with a smile. This simple facial expression is a double-edged sword. Should one be somewhat down a forced smile will turn inwards and will, at one point permeate your subconsciousness. On the other hand when one feels an intrinsic feeling of joy this will show itself on our faces in the form of a smile.

Laughter takes this process a step further. Have the dark clouds descended during your sleep and cannot be dispersed on waking: get up, go to the bathroom, look in the mirror and laugh. By the way singing serves the same purpose. The difference being that laughter follows the external – internal route and singing creates an internal arousal without necessarily influencing the external modus first.

Good, having cleared that up we shall continue with today's topic which is the inappropriateness of laughter when a smile would suffice and in some cases when even an external smile is inadvisable and inner mirth should be the preferred option.

Exempli gratia: when one is at a funeral it would be inappropriate to laugh when the priest says: "ashes to ashes, dust to dust". The great Irish comedian, Dave Allen was capable of solemnity and hilarity in his sketches but this talent has not been endowed on the majority of

human beings.
Another time and place when an inner grin should be given preference over laughter is at the dentist's. This obviously is also a preservation of one's health. Bursting into laughter just as the drill hits a nerve may not have the desired effect on the person using the aforementioned tool. Per viam, this also applies to visits to doctors especially urologists and gynaecologists.
A certain reticence would also be advisable while going about one's daily affairs outside the domestic environment. From personal experience I have learnt that it is inappropriate to laugh when confronted by five Hell's Angels asking you for a light.
In conclusion it can be said that although laughter really does help the medicine go down -paraphrasing Julie Andrews- there are times when an inner smile would be preferable to in-situ laughter. Next week we will be discussing the effects that our happy moods have on the people around us and those who we come into contact with on a daily basis.
Hopefully I will have been discharged from hospital by then and can welcome you once again from the comforts of my own front room. Till then: Keep smiling.

The Pact

Bill and Judy had been married for almost sixty years. Every morning Bill would fetch two cups of tea and they'd drink them in bed sitting side by side. They would then spend ten minutes in each other's arms. This moment of intimacy was sufficient for both of them. They'd always enjoyed the physical side of their relationship which, obviously, with the onset of old-age had become dramatically less, but they refused to give up these ten minutes.

Today they'd lain there in silence each busy with their own thoughts. A week beforehand had seen them at their local hospital. Their G.P. had wanted Judy to have some tests done as he didn't trust the complaints which she'd come to see him about. She was put through a whole rigmarole of tests: blood, urine, heart, pancreas and one or two more. She was prodded here, there and everywhere and they wired her up to a funny looking contraption which emitted a low whirring sound. All this time Bill was at her side, a silent assuring presence. Today they were to hear the results and Bill didn't want to share his worries with Judy just as Judy had decided to keep her fears to herself.

Their appointment was at three o'clock in the afternoon and at twenty past three they were back in the car holding hands and crying. After sixty years of sharing life, love, difficult moments and happy times, the diagnosis meant they would soon be split up. Bill tried to comfort his wife but he himself was distraught. He could not foresee a life without his Judy.

Surely this must be the epitome of true love when two people, each with their own unbearable suffering, still try to comfort the other person.

The went through the motions of driving home, making dinner and watching East Enders, preparing for the night, a goodnight kiss and eyes closed.

In the morning Bill fetched the two cups of tea which they drank in silence. It was only when they were embedded in each other's arms that they could find the words they needed to say. As is often the case the stronger of the two started: "Bill, three months isn't that long and to be honest I've suffered enough pain. I just want to call it a day. Remember that couple we became friends with on holiday last year? The ones that told us about those pills you could order on the internet? Well, last night, while you were asleep, I went on-line and ordered a box of those pills".

Bill felt the trickle of tears on his chest. At that moment he really wanted to support his wife but he felt as if he was submerging in quicksand. He needed her badly but he also realised he had to man up. He had the woman whom he loved more than anything else in the world in his arms but he himself felt like a babe in arms and within three months she would be taken away from him. His feelings of sadness and anger overwhelmed him. From somewhere deep down he managed to find the words he would never have dreamt of expressing. He suddenly realised that all the laws, morals and principles meant absolutely nothing. He had one light in his life and that was soon to be extinguished. "Judy, I'm not letting you go on your own. What have we always had as our motto? *Out together, home together.* Next Thursday is our wedding anniversary. That gives us time to get our things in order. Early in the evening we'll drive to our favourite beauty spot near the beach, take the pills and watch the moon come up. Please don't refuse me this". He felt more tears on his chest. Words were superfluous. All that needed to be said had been said.

The following three days were spent cleaning the house, checking all their paperwork viz. funeral insurance, testament etc. and writing a letter to their two children:

Dear Charlotte and Jimmy,

Your mom and I have decided that it's time to put our affairs in order and put this life behind us. Your mother has been in considerable pain the last six months and the doctor at the hospital has said she only has three more months left to live. I can't bear the thought of being without her and so we've decided to take that walk down death's aisle together.

I'm sorry we haven't spoken for a couple of years. We made our choices and it's a shame you couldn't accept them. You are still often in our thoughts and we shed the occasional tear when the birthday cards are returned. We've left everything equally to the two of you. The house is worth a bit at least.

We realise that what we are about to do will not help in reducing any animosity you feel towards us, but it's a choice we have made based on our mutual love.

Goodbye. We love you,
Daddy and Mommy

The morning that the package arrived was an awkward moment but Bill took hold of Judy's hands and looked into her eyes: it is good, was the unspoken message between them.

Thursday arrived and began with the inevitable cups of tea and embrace.

Once dressed they went down the local for a celebratory anniversary lunch and then went home to say goodbye to their house. Making sure that the gas and electricity had been switched off they locked up and walked hand-in-hand to the car.

It was an hour's drive and although Bill's hands were steady on the wheel his voice shook. Judy sat in the passenger seat resigned and at peace. Their individual thoughts were strangely aligned: their first kiss, their wedding day, the birth of the twins, the daily ups and

downs. The sixty years had literally flown by leading to this final trip together.
Little did they know that just over the hill, hurtling towards them on the wrong side of the road was a lorry whose driver had fallen asleep at the wheel.

The Operation

Her own G.P., the specialist, the anesthesiologist and also the nurse who welcomed her to the ward all spoke of a minor operation. To someone like Sybil, to whom having a splinter removed was tantamount to a major operation, this was not comforting. She was also a person who never touched a drop of alcohol nor indulged in any recreational drugs. This simply due to the fact that she had been disgusted watching herself the few times she had been inebriated. She also preferred to use meditation to sort out the workings of her inner mind. She had no qualms at facing her demons but she didn't want them taking control in a drug-induced stupor. And now here she was on the verge of voluntarily giving up control to Propofol, Ketamine or Etomidate. Google had furnished her with the pros and cons of anesthetics and the anesthesiologist had tried to put her mind at rest, alas to no avail. She had thought about refusing the operation but the consequences of such a decision were quite tricky. She now lay immobile on a table with a gigantic light searching out all her physical imperfections surrounded by masked nurses and doctors who were trying to put her at ease. They, however, were fully dressed and invisible behind their masks. She felt naked and vulnerable.

Following instructions she counted to ten while the anesthetic was injected into her veins. Looking back she thought she managed to get to five. She was at peace giving the scalpel and the suctures chance to do their work.

The literal term is being put to sleep. If major surgery has to be performed an extra drug is added to ensure that the patient is fully unconscious. During minor operations less invasive narcotics are used

thus inducing a dream-like state. Sybil found herself in dreamland.
She was standing at a fountain in Ancient Greece when an elderly beggar carrying a lantern walked by rapidly. Sybil had been a curious person her whole life and therefore she followed him and finally caught up with him at the steps of the Parthenon. He was involved in a heated argument with Plato, the philosopher, who was pompously trying to define a human being in the simplest terms possible. Every definition was parried by the beggar until Plato furiously cried out: "you stink like a mangy cur but you argue like a human being, ergo you are human". The beggar reiterated: "these men smell of lavender yet they have the interests of dogs, ergo they cannot be human beings". Sybil soon tired of this cock-fighting and turned to leave. Suddenly she eyed the date on a newspaper behind a window: 1913. A smartly-dressed gentleman approached her and said: "My dear lady, you have an exterior and an interior personality. Your past, present and future are all one and your libido is a psychic manifestation of your soul. Be the person you are".
Again she turned to walk away but found herself on a black couch in a darkened room. A small table lamp was visible and the outline of a youngish man sat close by observing her. Strangely she felt at peace and didn't want to talk. The man spoke with a Scottish twang and said: "your fear is your greatest enemy. You will only achieve hyper-sanity by first experiencing sheer madness. Treat it as a friend and it will show you the way to the light".
Sybil was suddenly caught up in a maelstrom of feelings. She heard the surgeon talking to one of the nurses about a film he'd seen two days beforehand. She wanted to shout out and let them know she was alive and listening, even though she was paralysed, but no sound came out of her throat. Instead the noise got caught in her throat and she started to choke. Eventually this sensation subsided but the fear didn't leave her.

And then she was once more ten years old and having her tonsils removed. The kindly matron was telling her she could wake up and the realisation hit her that her whole life from ten onwards had been but a dream and that she'd have to live through it all again. "No!", she cried out, "no! no! no…".
She felt a hand on her shoulder and an angelic voice saying: "You're all right Sybil. The operation was successful, come back to the land of the living". She opened her eyes and focusing, saw that she was in the recovery room and the nurse who had taken her into theatre was looking down at her smiling, holding a glass. "Come on, love, try and drink some water and we can return you to the ward".
Sybil was back in the present but she remembered her dreams vividly: Diogenes, Carl Jung, Laird, her fears, her anxieties. What was their message? Was she going insane? Or were these signposts pointing her in the right direction? Only time would tell and Sybil consciously decided to store them away until she was safely tucked up in her own bed, in her own apartment. Only then would she take them out – one by one – and try to learn the lessons they wanted to teach her.
Three hours later the surgeon who had operated her did his rounds. He stopped to talk to Sybil. He spoke in a friendly way, as a colleague:
"In a way, we're both alike", he said. "We both try and cure our patients".
"The difference being that I need thirty minutes whereas you need months, sometimes years. Maybe one day I'll require your services. Should that be the case I can only hope and pray that your operation will be as successful as mine was. You can go home tomorrow but make an appointment to see me in a fortnight's time. You were a wee bit restless during the operation, which is perfectly normal. Just try and get a good night's rest and you'll feel as right as rain".
Sybil knew she would never again be the same person she was before the operation. But she kept this knowledge to herself.

Two Children Please.

2066

Hannah and Hugo were born in the same year hence their similar initials. It was now thirty-two years since the inception of naming children born in the same year with the same initial. Their first child, if permission were to be granted, would be given a name starting with the letter K. Not that they would have any say in the matter. The Registration of Official Births' Office would supply them, at the onset of pregnancy, with two names beginning with the letter K, a boy's name and a girl's name. Five years earlier they had registered as prospective parents and today they were to receive official notification on whether or not they met the required standards to become parents and how many children they would be allowed to have.

Two months ago they had been sent the necessary documents which they had to fill in and return within thirty-six hours. These documents included an eight-page questionnaire on their background, education, hobbies and physical and mental stability. They also had to include five references, two of whom needed to be from people who knew them in a professional capacity e.g. teachers or doctors etc. There were also three forms which they both had to sign: a non-divorce agreement, a parental responsibility affidavit and a financial undertaking agreement.

This was the first hurdle. The second was a three-day stint at a Government Research Institution for the physical and mental capability tests. These tests ranged from sperm counts, uterus capacity, full medical check-ups and a whole day of psychiatric tests. The procedure was nearly called to a halt when Hugo professed an interest in thrice-weekly sex instead of the once a week norm but it was put down to youthful exuberance and a high energy count quite often found in men who were disposed to taking part in grueling sporting events.

A week later they received the good news and a letter in which the remaining procedure was explained. A Review Board would consider their application and a final decision would be made and sent to them on the date mentioned in the letter, which was today. At 10.20 exactly their digital mail box in the front room lit up and a mechanical voice filled the room: "Dear Hannah and Hugo, your application to be allowed to become parents has been granted. You are allowed to produce two children within a time frame of three years. We have made a hospital appointment for Hugo to have his anti-conception chip removed. Please present yourself at the Government Hospital at 3p.m. today. We advise you to start the conception procedure as soon as possible and to inform the proper authorities when aforementioned conception has taken place. Enjoy".

They were over the moon. At last they could join the ranks of modern-day parents.

2025

That the Labour Party had won the election was no surprise. The fact that they only had two major themes in their manifesto was a surprise: crime and unemployment. The Conservatives had won and lost the country on Brexit. Overjoyed at having once again regained control of their country, within a couple of years it had turned sour. The Eastern Europeans were still taking the jobs, prices had risen astronomically, poverty levels which wouldn't have seemed amiss in the time of Queen Victoria, Scotland had voted for , and gained, independence and were now a member of the E.U. with a border running parallel to Hadrian's Wall and the patience of the people in Northern Ireland had finally run out and they had signed an economic pact with the Republic of Ireland, cutting themselves off from the U.K and remaining tied to the E.U. Both Scotland and Northern Ireland had profited enormously from their choices whereas England, and its satellite state, Wales, were on the verge of bankruptcy. Not only was poverty rife but the crime rate had also rocketed.

With a working majority of 85% the Labour Government got to work immediately. They realised that it would take almost a generation to turn the ship around and therefore their first Legislation was to push through a constitutional change which meant they could rule for ten years without calling an election. The Bills passed through Parliament at a hitherto unprecedented speed. Trade agreements were signed with Russia, China, Cuba and Brazil which helped to finance the changes sought after by the Government. Within three years the following Acts of Parliament had been implemented:

The Criminal Exodus Act: all foreign nationals arrested and found guilty of committing a crime of any sort, would be returned to their country of origin. This would apply not only to recent migrants but it would go back five generations. The results were staggering. Inner-city gangs ceased to exist, young girls were no longer being groomed by Pakistani taxi drivers, women would safely walk the streets without fear of being raped by migrant workers and senior citizens once again took to meeting up in town centres.
The negative effects of these deportations were countered by The Employment For All Act. Benefits were removed and unemployment became the new crime. English people were now put to work harvesting, waitering, driving taxis and buses, garbage collecting and in the construction industries. Obviously there were protests initially but a month without any income soon persuaded the majority to accept their new lives.
Inner city housing became a focal point of change and almost at the blink of an eye modern tenement blocks were scattered around the city and a Minister of Domestic Bliss had been appointed to promote harmony in these new districts.
The third Act: The Parental Guidance Act was the most intrusive of all the new legislation and took many years before it was fully implemented. Research had shown that boys of single parent families were more likely to fall along the wayside. For the then Prime Minister, himself a father of five children, this was totally unacceptable and a failure of parental responsibility. His Bill encountered fierce opposition but, ultimately all M.P.s agreed that a radical change was the only hope and the Bill passed through both Houses with a minimum of fuss. The main points were that all boys had to have an anti-conception chip implanted at birth. This allowed sexual pleasure without the consequences - even though written permission from the female partner had to be obtained before intercourse took place. As children were the life-blood of society only those endowed

with good parenting skills within a marriage-based union would be allowed to procreate. To prevent a two-tier system in which only the rich would have the financial means to procure a procreation license, all applications would be dealt with by the Home Office and its subsidiaries in all major English cities. Every couple after five years of marriage were entitled to apply for official parenthood. The costs would be met by the Government, heavily subsidised by Chinese investments.

A new Golden Age was dawning on the dwindling British Isles.

2066

Hannah was relieved that Hugo had not insisted that she accompany him to the hospital. In one or two northern cities there had been a recent spate of hate attacks by women who weren't allowed to have children. Usually these attacks were carried out by divorcees under the influence of alcohol or couples who were proven to be incompatible. The Government had acted swiftly but nevertheless it was a sign of the times. As was alsothe latest Government Bill: The Puberty Financial Act. Undoubtedly there was equality among the classes concerning permission to procreate, however, low income families would no longer receive free education once their children had reached puberty as they were needed for the menial tasks in society.

In old history books Hannah had seen pictures of unarmed Bobbies patrolling the streets. That must have been a wonderful time she thought to herself. The armed Chinese soldiers standing at many of the cities' junctions and main buildings were not at all friendly. In fact she never felt at ease once she was outside their own compound.

She was glad that Hugo belonged to a professional class and that their compound was a safe haven guarded by members of the New English Security Company. It was even being whispered that there would soon be possibilities of travelling abroad. Obviously permission would be required from the Foreign Office and not everyone would be able to afford these holidays. The Government had proclaimed that they would not tolerate a resurgence of mass tourism abroad as preliminary talks had started with Europe and these must not be jeopardised by hordes of English yobs.

Tonight she would prepare Hugo's favourite meal and they'd open the bottle of wine they'd been saving. Before going into the kitchen she'd shower and shave and their romantic evening would start when Hugo got home. Their K was on its way.

The End of the Road

It suddenly dawned on him that he had tumbled over the edge of old age. In his dreams he could see the fork in the road. The left hand-one lead downwards to misery, bitterness, cynicism and decrepitude; the right- hand one lead upwards to strife, stillness, satisfaction and joy. At the end of both pathways was the same door marked "death". Behind the door the same peacefulness existed but on the left path the door was locked and one had to scream and shout and plead and knock on the door till one's knuckles bled. At the end of the right-hand path the door was open and a light was burning. A further difference was that as one descended, the path taken disappeared and an invisible energy pulled one inexorably towards the door marked death. The ascending path, however, always gave a panoramic view of the climb that had been made. From the first step far below on the shore, leading up through the forests and bare hillocks. The diversions that were taken, the circuitous routes, all could be seen. Also the places were stones had been taken out of the rucksack and dropped at the side of the road. Silent mounds with a plaque on top, witnesses to the struggles one had faced and learnt to cope with. The plaques shone brightly in the sun bringing a smile to the lips of the observer. A deep-rooted feeling of satisfaction at the climb taken was ingrained, etched even, into the soul.

He knew intuitively which path to take. The one he'd been on all his life. On the shore there had also been a choice of two paths: the easy one, which would eventually guide the traveller to the left-hand fork and the right hand one leading upwards. He read the notice board at the foot of the hill: "to take this road means an acceptance of not only the hardships but also the immense pleasure it will bring. Signposts will guide you but no one will support you. Perseverance must be your walking stick and love must be your nourishment. Be prepared to run the gamut of emotions and feelings but the rewards will also be yours."

He awoke with the dream still vivid in his mind and the day rushed in.

Yesterday she had packed all her clothes and today she would return for her remaining proof of their life together. Yes, it had run its course and although the relationship had enriched them both, he instinctively felt it was time to continue on his journey upwards.

In the beginning the 15-year age difference hadn't seemed an insurmountable problem. She was an old soul and his youthful exuberance hadn't deteriorated. Unfortunately with the passing of time they no longer complemented each other and she wished to retain the happy memories he had given her. Her fears that she would end up being his nurse was the proverbial straw. They had talked and cried and hugged and he had let her go.

With tears in his eyes but with a sanctuary lamp burning at the back of his mind, he reread the poem he had written before falling asleep last night. He looked out of his window and thought he saw a raven perched on the house opposite, but that was impossible. The dirge playing in his mind while he read was a musical accompaniment to his inner monologue.

The End

Birdie, birdie, flying in the air.
Spring or summer, you really don't care.
The cat is preying and you are the prayer.
Don't come down, you'll be safer up there.

Pussy, pussy, prowling around,
your eyes in the air and your feet on the ground.
Keeping watch, a silent mound.
Cautiously waiting, hearing every sound.

Telephone ringing, she's not coming home.
Her bags are packed and there's a flight to Rome.
She needs some time to be alone;
Pizza, spaghetti and a chicken's wish-bone.

The house is empty and the bed is cold.
Every day the mirror grows old.
The charm, the body, the strength so bold.
The book is closed the story's been told.

Wine, spirits, cigarettes and beer,
Every memory a falling tear.
The bird flies from the cat in fear.
Looking out the window but no one comes near.

Essay on "Roots"

There's no such thing as blue blood, or black blood or red blood, there's only the blood that runs through your veins via the umbilical cord. This blood came from the air your mother breathed and with each inhalation came particles of history. Blood shared by generation after generation, true blood. That is why to deny your background is tantamount to denying yourself. You are your ancestors and you are the future generations. Your place of birth may be arbitrary, your genes are not. Did your forefathers live in poverty? It doesn't mean that you are a poor person. Were your ancestors Lords of the Manor? That doesn't imply that you have a rich personality. We are all what we were meant to be. If a tree has the roots of an oak it will never become a Birch, not even if it is planted in a birch forest. This commonplace fact also applies to humans.

Neanderthals were tribal people not unlike modern-day man who clings to his nationality. A sense of identity is looked for within the group. What would happen if we relinquished national identity and we all became world citizens? Could the embracing of a nationality be the result of a lack of inner self-awareness or inferiority?

Kieran had been hard at work on his essay for the last three hours as it had to be handed in this afternoon. Their teacher had given them the title "Roots" and told them to write a 500 word essay. He knew what was expected of him but what a boring way to pass the morning. He could have been out on his racing bike or practicing on his guitar. He just hoped that his teacher wouldn't put it through the plagiarism scanner.

The assignment was based on a social science lesson about migration, or was it emigration? He should have paid more attention instead of staring at Helen's bare waist-line two desks in front of him. God that girl is mega-sexy. He looked at his watch and saw that he only had an hour to finish this stupid thing. Where's his mother with the tea and biscuits?

A tree and a person can be uprooted. If a tree is uprooted it dies but a human being doesn't. Can each countries' melting-pot absorb all new- comers? If that is the case why are there these global Black Lives Matter protests and demonstrations? The Afro-Americans were uprooted but apparently they weren't integrated. On the other hand Donald Trump saw himself as the All-American Guy but he was descended from German immigrants. Why were some thrown into the melting-pot and others into the fire?

Oooh, that was catchy. Old Walrus will like that. He had to include something about the States as O.W.'s boyfriend was a Yank. Imagine two men in bed together! Gross! It's alright down in London but up north you'd be more inclined to get a taste of Geordie manliness. You wouldn't need mascara with two black eyes.

The saying is: to put down roots – not new ones mind you. When a person migrates they take their roots with them. Sticking to the analogy of the forest, when someone from say England moves abroad and settles in another country, they don't turn into, for example, Germans. They remain an English tree in a German forest.
The question begs to be asked whether migration has positive benefits or negative consequences? As is usually the case there are two sides to the coin. When you're white, wealthy and educated and voluntarily migrating the benefits would far outweigh any negative effects. Should you on the other hand be forced to move – for economic reasons, or because of war, persecution, drought, famine or even slavery – and you do not in any way mirror the inhabitants of that particular country, the consequences could be dire.

This sounds intelligent, Kieran thought to himself, time to round it off. He was glad he would be allowed to drop the subject next year. At least then he'd have the chance to concentrate on more important subjects such as English, math and economics. Why do you need to know about migration if your aim is to become a car salesman? When he wasn't thinking about Helen he often contemplated on the absurdity of the things he had to learn at school. Okay, so William landed in Hastings in 1066. So what? The only time he goes down south is if Newcastle play an away game down there.

My opinion is that although nationality can lead to tribal attitudes with far-reaching consequences it does put a label on our roots. Our lineage, however, is far more important when describing who we are. There will always be migration and maybe therefore a global identity is a thing to strive for. This could, and I must emphasize "could", put a stop to discrimination, abuse, trafficking and the other unwanted results of turmoil in poorer parts of the world.

Yes! Finished! Kieran thought to himself with twenty minutes to spare. I'll give Helen a ring and ask how she's getting on with her assignment. I might even offer to help her.

Breaking News

Making History

Today two historic events took place simultaneously in London. Parliament Square was renamed The Emily Pankhurst Square. This renowned suffragette has finally earned her rightful place in history. In The Houses of Parliament the new M.P. for Dudley West, Ms. Arjita Bharati was making her maiden speech following her by-election victory.

2066 will become known as the year in which for the first time ever, The House of Commons has a 100% female membership and Ms. Bharati's speech, the shortest in living memory echoed the reality of the day: "Ladies, we've done it".

Outside, demonstrations were taking place both of supporters of an all-female House as also those who deplored the idea. These two groups highlighted the differences in our country. Highly-educated women bearing placards which read: "Veni-vidi-vici", or "Feminism is Democracy" or "Gender is irrelevant. Commonsense has prevailed". On the opposite side of the square braying men bearing hand-written signs such as: "F-off. Back on your backs" was one of the more prosaic efforts. The others being barely legible. A huge police presence was needed to keep the two sides at bay.

Congratulating Ms.Bharati the Prime Minister concluded her speech in a crowded House of Commons with the words: "leaps and bounds have been made in our emancipation struggle. It is now time for male suffrage. We must work towards this end to prevent any more fissures in our society. In the next few years priority must be given to building bridges across the clefts and crevices which have appeared. We need the men to take on their responsibility. We shall lead them along the path, a joint venture for the good of all. Thank you".

A roaring cheer rose up from the House which was audible to the two factions outside.

Mary Glynnis-Smythe. Home Editor at the BBC.